Believe!

Carol Davios

BRIGHTEST
CHRISTMAS
WISHES!
Jan Rasmssen

D1237404

A Door County
Night Before Christmas

ISBN 978-0-9905985-0-3

Register of Copyrights, United States of America

Copyright 2014 by From Door to Door Publishing.

Printed in the U.S.A.

Third Printing

www.adoorcountynightbeforechristmas.com

Twas the night before Christmas and a blanket of snow,

Had given Door County a sparkling glow.

The stockings were empty
but the kids' hopes were high,

They'd be filled up with presents
when Santa stopped by.

The children were
sleeping all tucked in
their beds,

While dreaming of
zipping
d
o
w
n
h
i
l
l
on their sleds.

Mama in her Packer scarf
and I in my socks,

We threw our coats on and
walked out to the dock.

When out in the cherry trees there rose such a clatter,

We ran in the snow to see what was the matter.

The Northern Lights shone on the wintry scene,
At 20 below, it looked like a dream!

There he was, arrayed in his glory,
The red sledding suit, well, it told the whole story.

His eyes were so happy,
his smile was merry,

He took a quick break
when he rode the car ferry!

His cheeks were like cherries – his beard almost froze,
He was thinking of ice fishing – "I suppose."

He had a pudgy face and a big round belly,

Loved Belgian Pies from a Door County deli.

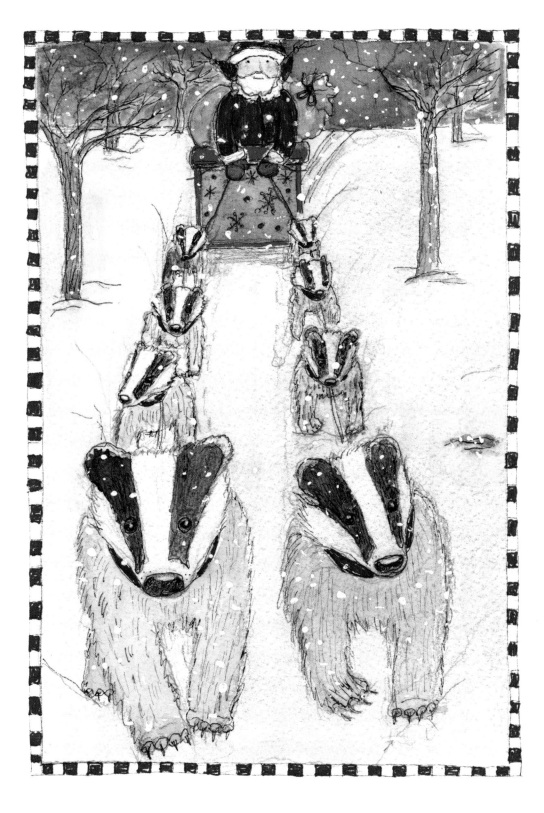

The badgers pulling
the sled full of gifts,

Knew how to navigate
all through the drifts.

Now Erik, now Elsa, now Gustav and Thor,

On Arvid, on Sven, on Inga and Bjorn.

Above Eagle Tower
and into the sky,

Go magic badgers
– zip by – fly high.

Then later that night all settled in bed,

I heard on my roof where those badgers did tread.

Down the chimney
Santa did slide,

Jumped off those coals
and came inside.

His sledding suit had
some ashes on it,

But his hat and his
scarf were not dirty
one bit.

His bundle of toys so large and so cheery,
Was heavy and full but did not make him weary.

His warm, knitted hat fit his round head just right,
His ears were all covered for a cold winter's night.

He did not speak much but went right to work,

Filled stockings –
gave presents – then
turned with a jerk.

Then up the chimney
he rose so quick,

I didn't get to see
what was his trick.

He jumped on his
sled and whistled to
his team,

Away they flew – this
had to be a dream.

High in the sky I heard a great sound,
"Merry CHRISTmas to All the world around!!"

Some Words of Explanation:

Cheese Curds - Solid parts of soured milk – "Squeaky Cheese" – found where there are cheese factories because ideally they need to be eaten within 12 hours of manufacture for the "squeak." Fresh curds squeak against the teeth when bitten into due to trapped air which escapes with time. A favorite food in Door County whether eaten alone or in meals. We have Renard's Cheese factory in Door County who is our largest supplier of cheese curds for Door County.

Cana Lighthouse – "Travel back in time and explore one of Door County Wisconsin's most popular lighthouses that's been standing watch on the shore of Lake Michigan for more than 140 years. Investigate the entire 8.7-acre island that includes the 89-foot-tall light tower, the original home of the lighthouse keeper and his family, and the oil house where fuel for the light was stored. The highlight of any Cana Island visit is climbing the 97 steps of the tower's spiral staircase to reach the gallery deck. The outside deck delivers a sweeping view of Lake Michigan and the Door County peninsula."
— www.dcmm.org

Hill 17 – Peninsula State Park – the #17 fairway at the park golf course is a favorite sledding spot. — dnr.wi.gov/topic

Green Bay Packers – "On Aug. 11, 1919, a score or more husky young athletes, called together by Curly Lambeau and George Calhoun, gathered in the dingy editorial room of the old Green Bay Press-Gazette building on Cherry Street and organized a football team. They didn't know it, but that was the beginning of the incredible saga of the Green Bay Packers." www.packers.com What more can we say? If you live in WI, you are a Packer fan – only a few exceptions!!

Cherries – "Door County prides itself on its cherry orchards, and a history of cherry growing that dates back to the 19th century. Soil and weather conditions… influenced by Lake Michigan and Green Bay have created an ideal environment for growing these fruits. Today (Door County has) around 2,200 acres of cherry orchards and another 1,000 acres of apple orchards."
— Wikipedia

"Nicknamed 'America's Super Fruit,' cherries are a delicious way to reap the health-promoting properties of antioxidants. Health and nutrition experts say to look no further than fruits grown in American soil for health and wellness benefits."
— wisconsincherries.org

Northern Lights – They do shine in Door County, but not every night. I, Carol, have personally seen them. I just pull over and watch the show!!

Badgers – The badger (taxidea taxus) was designated the official Wisconsin State animal in 1957.

Scandinavian and Belgians in Door County – "Today, Door County's heritage can be experienced through our many museums, lighthouses, tours, and historic sites, as well as our people. From the Belgians in the south to the Scandinavians in the north, from trippe to fish boils, from maritime to farm museums, Door County honors its past by preserving the best of its traditions, foods, buildings, and artifacts." For more information, contact the Door County Visitor's Bureau at (920) 743-4456. — www.doorcounty.com

Besides, talking about Scandinavian names, Carol's friend and neighbor is Arvid!!

Eagle Tower – Located inside Peninsula State Park.

Car Ferry – Washington Ferry Line – operates year round. "When you reach the end of Highway 42, at the tip of Wisconsin's Door County peninsula, you'll find Northport Pier and the Washington Island Ferry Line. The Washington Island Ferry Line was started in 1940 with two existing wooden ferries. Over the years steel ferries were added and today the line boasts modern, Coast Guard-approved vessels that make up to 25 round trips a day during high season and two round trips per day in winter. After vehicles and passengers are safely on board at the Northport ferry dock, the ferry will embark on a 30-minute ride past Plum, Pilot and Detroit Islands. This area is filled with history. You will be making the same passage as the Native Americans who paddled their canoes from island to island, French explorers who came to the area and schooners that traveled this passage a century ago. Relax and enjoy the ride!" — wisferry.com/about-us/

Ice Fishing – "Ice fishing is the practice of catching fish with lines and fish hooks or spears through an opening in the ice on a frozen body of water. Ice anglers may sit on the stool in the open on a frozen lake, or in a heated cabin on the ice, some with bunks and amenities." — en.wikipedia.org

"I suppose" – common saying in Door County.

Belgian Pies – (In) "the 1880s, the hard-working Belgians began celebrating their bountiful harvests with a tradition known as Kermiss. Kermiss is still celebrated today on the third Sunday of September. The women of the area serve homemade Belgian pies and waffles, Trippe made of sausage, pork and cabbage, a pork and cabbage side dish called Jutt, and a traditional soup made of chicken and vegetables called Chicken Booyah." www.doorcounty.com Today you can buy Belgian Pies any day in Door County from many local bakeries and delis.

Christmas – The day we celebrate the birth of Jesus Christ, Son of God.

To help celebrate Door County, we have hidden a small door with a spiral door knob in each picture page within this book. Have fun looking for all the Doors!

Carol Davis lives with her wonderful husband, Steve and feels blessed to live in such beautiful place as Door County, WI. Carol is a grief counselor in Door County and a writer. She has published a book called "Aloha," about sharing your legacy. She has four children, three whom live in the Green Bay area, and one in PA. At this time she has two wonderful grandsons. She enjoys being outdoors, reading, writing and quilting. This book was written for all of us who still believe.

Jan Rasmussen and her family have lived in Door County for 14 years. She loves and appreciates being able to live in such a beautiful place all year round. She enjoys art, writing, cooking, reading and all the things that Door County has to offer.